The Moribund Portal

The Moribund Portal

Spectral Resonance & the Numen of the Gallows

Richard Gavin

THREE HANDS PRESS
2018

ADMONITION TO THE READER

The Gallows, Gibbet and Hanging Tree, as instruments of death, are uniquely dangerous testaments to the horrors of humanity. Their accreted folklore and symbolism are the especial subjects of this book. Neither the author nor publisher advocate, nor accept responsibility for, the illegal or harmful actions of any parties resulting from abuse of these infernal machines.

First Three Hands Press edition 2018.

ISBN 9781945147241 (softcover)

Cover image by Benajmin A. Vierling.
Interior book and cover design by Joseph Uccello.
Fine edition designs by Daniel A. Schulke.

Printed in the United States of America.

www.threehandspress.com

Other works by Richard Gavin

FICTION COLLECTIONS

Charnel Wine

Omens

The Darkly Splendid Realm

At Fear's Altar

Sylvan Dread: Tales of Pastoral Darkness

ESOTERICISM

The Benighted Path: Primeval Gnosis and the Monstrous Soul

AS EDITOR

Penumbræ: An Occult Fiction Anthology
(co-edited with Daniel A. Schulke & Patricia Cram)

SITES OF ARCHAIC tragedy, iniquity, or turmoil can serve the living as stations of unique spirit function. Though the haunted ambience of such localities may be only faintly perceived by some visitors and not at all by others, their eerie character does acutely claim those who approach such areas with receptivity and an appreciation of the gravity of the pacts that can be forged there. The powers indigenous to forlorn places may be subtle, yet they are anything but tenuous.

Ghostly infusions of the land billow between worlds, that of the grosser material plane and that of the immaterial numen which infuses material forms with their essential meaning, their soul if you will. However, before one can even perceive indwelling spirits a perceptual distention within the observer must first occur. This reorientation may well transform one's mere glimpse of shimmer or shade into a robust purview of the realm of the Dead. But such reorientation requires a formidable degree of preparatory reflection, endeavour, and daring. One must not only prove one's worthiness, but also their willingness to go beyond boundaries, both internal and external. While the specifics of such an ordeal will vary according to an individual's ken, affinities, and geographic location, the underlying essence is uniform. Indeed, Spectral Resonance is a phenomenon as radiant and precise as the firmament of the heavens.

To participate in Spectral Resonance is to serve as the flesh-and-blood component of a pact with the non-corporeal. One must therefore orient their perceptual fields toward the phantom realm; a realm that is customarily experienced only in the merest and most evanescent of encounters. This timeless substratum, this demimonde, will herein be distinguished as 'the Otherworld.' For while this teeming Otherworld does exist outside the empirical world, it is only *just* outside, a degree or two beyond the pale. The slightest wayward act, the quiescence to afford unhindered subconscious reverie, the bout of silent contemplation; all such techniques erode the transitory veils that blind us to the Otherworld. While complete immersion into this plane carries the tariff of one's very life, the living may nonetheless interact with the Otherworld by the hard-won attainment of a state of visionary receptiveness. This rarefied form of soul-repose is the crucial aspect that affords the living the gift of Spectral Resonance.

Be it the peripheral glimpsing of a nocturnal apparition, the recognition of a previously-experienced omen that re-manifests as *déjà vu*, or the intuited nearness of an unseen presence that makes itself known through the icy raising of one's hackles, these uncanny incidents are intrinsically at odds with the utilitarian/materialistic lens that the bulk of humanity has been trained to filter reality through since the era of the so-called Enlightenment in eighteenth century Europe. This obsession with empirical evidence and a mechanistic view of the universe has since became the de facto paragon of wisdom. Hence, Otherworldly encounters are reflexively reduced by the modern mind. They are believed to be rare flashes, flukes, exceptions to the glittering norm of rationality. It is little wonder then that many who have such experiences immediately dismiss them as quirks of the human brain, as nothing but sensorial trickery.

Emancipation from this linear assessment of the real will lead one to the unshakable revelation that our world is perennially haunted, that the Sabbat of gods and spirits occurs unceasingly, everywhere, in all things.

Those who seek to catalogue, analyze, or outright dismiss the Otherworld are akin to the lepidopterist pinning lifeless moths to corkboard; they may study, even admire, the specimens they have collected, but these specimens are only husks, shells that are devoid of the deep, vibrant meaning they once radiated. Such necrotic tactics are ones of reification, an effort to draw the spiritual experience into the paradigm of materialism. In such models, intimations of the Otherworld must either conform to the mechanics of systems designed to assess the observable functions of the material universe (whose results must be repeatable) or they will be discarded.

To cultivate Spectral Resonance, one does not strive to reify the hidden presences that dwell on the far side of the Veil. Instead the aspirant *rarefies his or her self*, and thereby grows attuned to the Otherworld. Spectral Resonance demands the adoption of a perceptual mode that is anathema to the 'civilized' worldview. The everyday consciousness of the modern man or woman is usually a dizzying tempest of personal memories, brief fantasies, and varying neuroses over the future. But these are the symptoms of the malady of linear time-reckoning. Most view time as an arrow whose past events are but pale, inert relics and whose present is but a blip doomed to dissolve in the wake of our race toward tomorrow. The so-called modern man or woman has no hope of ever achieving Spectral Resonance so long as they cleave to the linear, progressive model of being.

To engage with the Otherworld, one must forge within themselves a primordial perspective. From this perspective the future dissipates into a mental abstraction, a product of the demiurge. Timelessness blossoms about one like a harmonic tone, a thunderclap that resounds between the two truly vital polarities of time: that of the past and that of the present. Within the timeless state, the past is not some wistful nostalgia of days gone by, but is a potent surge, an eruption from the Underworld, the realm that is teeming with the magisteries of the hidden, the fleshless horde that is composed of both ancestors and unfamiliars.

The complexion of the present is also profoundly altered by the primordial perspective, evolving from a brief tick of the clock that one scarcely notices into a living, brimming nexus of reception where one's cup runs over with the sensation of *in-betweenness*.

Once one finds their psyche oscillating between the distant past and the scintillating present, their circle of operation waxes into the Moribund Portal, luminous and spirit-enthused. The Portal is the rim of the chthonic cauldron that churns with one's own blood-memory. When in the proximity of the Moribund Portal, one becomes a rarefied being, a witness to that which cannot be seen with the mortal eye. They are suspended between two worlds, much like the mythic image of the Hanged Man with his copious secrets. Hence the Moribund Portal's deep connection to the gallows.

Measures must be taken by each visitor to ensure that they are able to attune themselves to the Hanging Place without becoming mired down in either its reputation or its historical significance in relation to social justice or injustice. To truly apprehend and appreciate the latent import of such places requires one to avoid being swayed by any vulgar lens. Instead one must adopt a dizzyingly elevated vantage, the perceptual eyrie wherefrom all phenomena is surveyed from a detached perspective, impervious to the taints of individual likes or dislikes, or to any social conditioning. This eyrie looms above the emotive and mental extremes. From this vantage, one perceives, even partakes, but is never consumed by the content of their metaphysical excursions. A person so rarefied is akin to the vultures and carrion crows that patiently circumambulate the Gallows, surveying the place entire, seeing all things from a position that slots them into their proper place. And like these avian scavengers, the esoterically-oriented visitant can intuit when the moment is right to approach, to partake or "feed upon" whatever essences thrum there. A quotient of this devoured essence is invariably carried back from this ghost-feast to the land of the quick.

While one may fall prey to fascination over the sheer morbidity of the gallows that has accreted over time (and now exudes like a thick autumnal fog) these baser drives must be transmuted into grist for the greater wheel that turns around these sites; the wheel that grinds simple gruesomeness into proteins. To those properly attuned, the macabre locality becomes a bastion of sacred power.

¶

SEARCH WELL YOUR *heartfelt intentions and weigh them scrupulously against your egoic drives. Test your very character.*

Then may you gather the totems germane to the horrors of the writhing Past and ignite the lamp of holy recurrence in the living Now.

Approach the crepuscular tree whose shadow veils the crossroads like the shroud upon the corpse.

Raise high the hangman's rope.

Breathe life into the bornless child of the poisonous root, the alraune spawned from the seed of strangulation.

Only by the casting of charnel signets, by the transmutation of ritual into a protracted convulsion, will the accursed place grant one the ability to witness and participate with the Moribund Portal.

When this occurs, all the bloodstained yesterdays shall bloom as

flowers, opening to reveal their buried sublimity.
The noose dangling vacantly from crooked bough shall frame the Portal. This is the astral lens through which one sees the Dead, and through which one is in turn seen by the Dead.

The imperishable numina that surround the gallows are innately elusive, thus to even attempt to sift through the lore of the Hanging Place with the aim of distinguishing its mystical underpinnings from its societal or moral entanglements is to run the risk of finding one's self equally entangled, like the very threads that wind to form the noose itself. Yet by pushing past the clatter and clutter that tethers the gallows to the mundane sphere, one soon finds themselves in eldritch country, the region of folk-belief and spirit-pacts.

¶

NOT FAR FROM where I sit writing these words there stands a hill that is well known to those versed in Canadian ghost lore. An account from the nineteenth century describes how this site came to bear the moniker of Gallows Hill. Upon this hill there once ran a primitive road which was flanked by sizeable banks of earth that had been forged by the excavations of the land.

Buttressed upon these clay banks was a great fallen tree whose genus has been lost to history. This tree is said to have been toppled by a raging thunderstorm and left to repose upon the banks, where it loomed like a misshapen canopy, just high enough above the road to allow wagons and wayfarers passage.

One summer evening in the 1800s a farmer was returning home from the market in York.[1] As his wagon negotiated the twilit hill, the farmer encountered a horrifying sight: from the tree's skein of limbs there hung a man. A noose was cinched taut about his neck. His face was livid and lifeless. The dangling corpse swung upon the blasted tree like a pendulum, drenched in the guttering shadow-play of the gloaming.

The farmer hastily reported the incident, but it came to nought. After leading the authorities back to the top of the hill he could find no sign of the hanged man. An official investigation was launched; lands were scoured, locals were questioned, missing persons were researched, but no clue was ever unearthed. To this day the identity of the hanged man remains unknown.

From that night onwards, this ruddy path with its fallen tree became known as Gallows Hill, a title that became a household word in Upper Canada and remained so for many subsequent decades.

To the historian, an account such as this might be taken as an old wives' tale, or a fragment whose banal explanatory details have simply been lost with the passage of time. But the fact remains that the locals allowed the road that ran upon Gallows Hill to fall into disuse.

1 York was the name settlers used for this segment of Ontario from 1793 until 1834, when a successful petition led to its name being changed to Toronto.

It was simply accepted throughout Upper Canada that Gallows Hill was a haunted place, a site where one was never truly alone.

Superstition can be defined as the irrational and unfounded belief in something of which one has no direct knowledge. Today this definition has become so loose and dismissive that there is an almost immediate impulse to lump all philosophical, mystical and matters of spirits into the same derogatory category, i.e. the folly of the unenlightened. It is this same impulse that feeds the linear, progressive model of time, through which our ancestors are dismissed as intellectually malnourished peasants who flinched at the sight of their own shadows and staggered about their primitive world like frightened hares, all because they lacked the luxuries and technological marvels of modernity.

While much could be said in critical response to this kind of contemporary solipsism, it is sufficient to draw the important distinction between superstition and genuine Spiritism.

Superstition is the ingrained trepidation that prevents one from undertaking certain activities for fear of negative repercussions. Such trepidation is often held by someone who has had no direct experience with these taboo deeds or thoughts. Theirs is a wariness to any endeavour they fear may result in punishment, be it physical or psychical. They toe the proverbial line in the hope of avoiding calamity. So while superstition does acknowledge some form of unseen, impersonal principles at work in the world, it is nevertheless based on a shrinking away from what they believe to be negative or overwhelming forces.

Spiritism, in contrast, is rooted in the deep bond between the incarnate and the disincarnated. This bond is forged by *direct experience* with a spirit or spirits and is strengthened by the individual's receptivity and responsiveness to them. While this may involve the departed ghosts of ancestors or loved ones, Spiritism is not relegated to personal reminiscences, nor is it purely emotive. While it may incorporate more ethereal phenomenon, such as trance or dream, Spiritism is not the mere by-product of psychophysical functioning.

Spirits and gods were woven into the fabric of ancient life not because of a lack of scientific knowledge, but because our ancestors lived in the larger world; one not designed by humanity. It was a bristling place, it was Nature entire, with all its merciless peril and untamed wonderment. The shelter that our ancestors forged from the living real was far thinner than the bubble within which modern humanity moves. What's more, the ancients comprehended this far more readily than modern folk do. The fierce, unveiled wilderness was just outside the door of those houses of wattles and daub. Night truly fell in those firelit villages. Darkness meant something to our ancestors.

Today we have lost this connection because we are quite literally addicted to light. We have washed out all developed areas with constant artificial illumination. Darkness is now often little more than an ambient backdrop to our nocturnal activities.

Authentic Spiritism is based on what the practitioner has seen with their own eyes, heard with their own ears, and in some cases, touched with their own hands. Though 'proving' the existence of the Otherworld is of interest only to the more data-minded 'ghost-hunters,' Spiritism has a wealth of 'data' to evidence its existence. But moulding the Otherworld to fit the narrow confines of objectivism is of no interest to the Spiritist. The proof of Spiritism remains ever-hidden from the profane. It reveals itself not through detached inquiry, but through the interaction of living image and the soul that bore witness to that image, and as well through solitary deed.

To dismiss or disparage Spiritism (particularly when the disparager has had no direct experience with spirits whatsoever) is more likely an expression of hubris than enlightenment. It is so facile to categorically deny the deeper aspects of the living wilderness when one spends one's life in climate-controlled, well-lit urban settings and surrounds themselves with likeminded acquaintances, all the while filtering the world through one digital screen or another.

Such a person's opinion may not be quite so ironclad were they to venture, alone and without the crutch of technology, into the savage wilderness, with only the glimmer of the moon to guide them to some nefarious space where the Hidden often slithers into view.

In the case of Ontario's Gallows Hill it was not superstition alone that distinguished this site. The numen of the Hanging Place staked a claim on that patch, for this lone incident transmuted the complexion of the hill and its tree. The nameless victim, the hanging with no discernable reason behind it, the dreadful discovery: such elements imbued Gallows Hill with the gifts of being a spectral way-mark. None could ever ascertain the specific nature of that lone sighting, yet many were endowed with a sense of that hill's mystery. Many could feel that it was a suggestive locale, a shadowy elsewhere, a borderland that pressed York firmly against the Otherworld.

What distinguishes the present work from the more broader surveys of hauntings and haunted places is that its focus is less on the ghostly residue that haunted locales may or may not be host to and is instead concerned with the rarefying dynamics that are indigenous to the gallows. The various empathic or investigatory elements that typically arise when exploring destinations that are reputedly haunted or cursed are of diminished importance here. While unearthing the historical data that buttresses the folklore connected to such areas is a worthwhile activity, my intention here is not to pinpoint the political or sociological aspects of the Hanging Place, but to emphasize its role in Spectral Resonance, in its ability to aid in the attuning of one's perceptions to the presencing that is so keenly felt there.

From its inception in medieval times, the gallows was infused with twin energies: that of the vulgar and that of the sacred. The word gallows, which was in use in English-speaking lands as early as the 13th century, is derived from the Proto-Germanic word *galgon*, meaning 'pole.' *Galgon* then underwent various modifications through Germanic and Old Saxon languages before eventually becoming pluralized as *galgen*, 'two poles.' While the intersecting poles in question are today often attributed to the Abrahamic cross of crucifixion upon Golgotha, the Christian presentation of this symbol is but a pale echo of older, deeper Mysteries of the Gothic peoples. In this instance, it was the Mysteries of the Gebo rune (X). This rune is the glyph of both sacrifice and union, of sexual congress and of the blessed nexus where the gods imbue humanity with seditious wisdom. Gebo is the rune of ecstasy, the surge of divine blood-Gnosis that eclipses all intellectual knowledge and transforms the recipient into the graal that brims with the nectar of the gods.

Here we see that while the form of the Hanging Place was shifted by the forces of history, culture, and geography, its two-pronged function—namely as being a tool of not merely execution but also sublimation—has been extant from its very inception.

Even the more ossified model of the Christ upon Golgotha presents elements that intertwine it with the topic at hand. Most notably, the presence of Dismas and Gestas, the penitent and impenitent thieves who were condemned alongside the messiah of Christian theology. Dismas was stationed at the Christ's right hand, and it was he who was the last of the worldly mortals to have accepted the Christ's alleged divinity and was thereby afforded admittance to the afterlife. Dismas, whose name meant 'evening' (again, evocative of the liminal, the in-between), sought absolution prior to his perishing.

Gestas exhibited something of a disaffected nature, which was wholly apt given his station at the left hand of god. He rebuked the claims of the Christ.

At noontide on the day of the crucifixion the sun was eclipsed by an unnatural blackness that draped Calvary in darkness for a trinity of hours, at which time Jesus unleashed his final cry. The ascension of both the Christ and Dismas is often symbolized by their vacated crosses atop Golgotha. Byzantine iconography commonly shows these crucifixes as the Suppedaneum Cross (☦), meaning that their design has not one but three horizontal crossbeams upon the ascending pillar. In this trio of beams, the topmost bears the Christ's title ('INRI') bestowed upon him by his persecutor Pontius Pilate, the second is where the Christ's arms were said to be pinioned, and the lowermost crossbeam represents a footrest for the crucified. As is the case with all symbolic lore, a cryptic inner significance can be teased out of this image of the lowermost beam.

Depending on whose crucifix is being depicted, the bottom beam may be sloping either downward to the left with its right butt tilting skyward, or vice-versa. Orthodox teachings claim that this positioning is a sign that the penitent thief did indeed ascend into heaven, for the lowermost crossbeam on the crucifixes of both the Christ and the penitent thief are tilting in the same direction, whereas the bottom beam of the cross of Gestas the Impenitent is tilted in the opposite direction;

an architectural insinuation that he was cast downward into the lower realms, the Underworld. Untameable Becoming was Gestas's eternal punishment for his lack of faith in the Christ's celestial promise.

In this model the lowermost crossbeam acts as a divine scale that gauges the meritorious 'weight' of a person's soul and determines the tone of their afterlife. The mythic origins of a process of that measured one's guilt or virtue upon death predate Christianity by millennia, having been an established tenet of the pantheistic faith of Egypt, where Anubis, the jackal-headed Lord of the Dead, would weigh the hearts of the newly deceased against the divine Feather of the goddess Ma'at. It can also be found in angelic lore with the archangel Michael, who measured the heft of sin inherent in the hearts of those seeking admittance to heaven. This is the reason why Michael is frequently depicted as clutching a sword in one hand and weighing scales in the other.

Judas Iscariot famously opted for the noose after the guilt over his treachery became too great to bear. The flowers that bloom upon the species of tree from which Judas hanged himself were said to have once been pure white, but on the day of his self-murder they turned red, becoming irrevocable emblems of the shame of betrayal. The cosmic hanging that is said to have occurred on the redbud tree has forever changed its name to the Judas Tree.

It behooves me to extract one final aspect from the Golgotha model. It can be obviously posited that in biblical doctrine Christ was believed to have been divine.

Therefore, of all the possible wretches or criminals that could have been with him at that pivotal moment of his crucifixion/transubstantiation why were thieves specifically singled out in this mythic model?

One layer of underlying significance in relation to this shall lead us beyond Biblical lore and into the curious marriage that seems to exist between divinity and thievery. After all, the Christian mythos is but a didactic and detrimentally literal regurgitation of the primordial Mystery of divinity sacrificed. But unlike its pagan forebears, Christianity is imbued with a transcendentalist cosmology, with the notion that the realm of the flesh is but a vile prison worthy only of derision and denial. Indeed, the essence of not only Christianity but indeed all Abrahamic thought is that there is an afterworld that is, unlike the Otherworld, wholly removed from the realm of the quick. What's more, this pain-free celestial kingdom of nullification should serve as the ultimate aspiration throughout one's terrestrial life.

Those possessing a more chthonic intuitiveness are aware that soul and skin are the true twin arms of the cross. To become the nexus where these poles meet is to experience the Gnostic-pagan reality of spirit-haunted matter, of soul enfleshed. This is the inkling of the luminous half-world, of the Hanging Place that is neither of the transcendent immaterial plane nor fully of the Earth. It is why the Hanging Place has served, both in mythical and in existential examples, as the mode of termination for god and thief alike.

The very concept of theft, pondered not from a societal or moralistic stance but from that isolated carrion-crow vantage affords impartial clarity and the ability to perceive deeper, subtle meanings, unveils numerous mystical principles of thievery that intimate its role in initiation. Prometheus famously stole the fire of the gods on Mount Olympus and bestowed it upon humanity so that they might illuminate in their divinity. This act of cosmic robbery disrupted the placid order of the universe and skewed humanity toward becoming creatures that were no longer mere clay but vessels that housed primal fire; cosmogonic flames that heated the blood through the imaginative faculty that allows us to comprehend realities deeper than apparent mirages.

A thief is one who takes that which is not rightfully his. In the profane world this translates into the absconding of material goods or coin of the realm. Yet if this selfsame act is presented as an aspect of a myth, a fairy-tale, or scrap of folklore, it becomes infused with rousing significances which the reader or listener disinters for their own enrichment. There is no mediator in such moments of Gnosis. They are enacted upon one's interiority, directly, like the lightning bolt forged in Tartarus that steers the fate of the cosmos.

Myth and folklore emanate from the occulted, radiant domain of gods and spirits, and therefore its themes, structure, and patterns are employed less for literary wholeness than as gateways through which one may commune with the submerged truth that churns beneath the surface of a given tale.

Such a theory is hardly novel to anyone possessing even a casual grasp of literary criticism. But the underlying principle, i.e. that the truth of any experience dwells beneath the surface of our conscious awareness, does extend far beyond the realm of the cultural theorist. It is in fact the quintessence of the numinous experience.

It may be that in certain tales the thief is the only truly just figure in a seemingly orderly but nevertheless unjust society. Much in the way that the archetypal Fool is often the keeper of crazy wisdom that is too heady for the commoner to bear, the thief's actions may be those of one who heeds a deeper or higher calling, a calling that emanates from somewhere beyond the land of men, a calling that renders these characters unfit for conventional living. Such figures become highway bandits crouching in the shadows, or hermits hiding in their hovels. They are the denizens of that wilderness that stretches ominously, unkempt and lawless, beyond the village's snug walls.

If caught and executed, in lore and in history, it was the corpse of the thief that would often be publicly displayed. From a tree or from the gallows at the land's border, their lynched cadavers dangled as a grisly example, a flaunting of judicial power, a warning to any other potential lawbreakers of what their fate would be.

Records of such tactics can be found as early as the writings of Herodotus (484 BCE–425 BCE), whose account 'King Rhampsinitus and the Robber'[2] describes

2 See *Histories* by Herodotus.

the scheming of a mason charged with the construction of a vault in which King Rhampsinitus could store his vast treasure. The mason secretly installs a moveable stone that will afford him access to the otherwise impenetrable chamber. On his deathbed he passes this secret on to his two sons, who then proceed to incrementally plunder the King's trove.

Baffled by this invasion of his seemingly intact chamber, the king orders that traps be laid to ensnare the clever burglars. His plan succeeds, for one of the brothers finds himself entangled in a trap during another of their nocturnal raids. The trapped thief orders that his brother decapitate him to avoid his identification by the king's men. The brother reluctantly obeys, and the following day Rhampsinitus orders that the mysterious headless cadaver be hung from the palace's outer wall so that any relatives who might come by to mourn would lead to the discovery of the thief's identity.

The power of the terminating gallows is that it wrings the apparent or the implicit into the suggestive, the shadow-form. The very word 'terminate' evokes this process, for its etymological roots stretch back to the Latin *terminus*, meaning 'boundary line.' Ancient Romans deified boundary lines as the god Terminus, to whom standing stones were erected on borderlands, stones that would be quenched in blood and other offerings made in reverence to the lord of liminalities.

One also finds the noose slung over similar waymarks of the perimeter, at the thin place that defines one land from another. In the mundane sense, such divisions can be found in the distinguishing of property. Strung mystically, the waymarks of Terminus serve as portals where two states of being can mutually ebb and flow.

Such has been the nature of hanging since the concept first entered human culture. The first known recorded instance of execution by hanging can be found in Book XXII of Homer's enduring work of mythopoeia, *The Odyssey*, which scholars estimate was written sometime during the eighth century BCE.

In this section of Homer's epic, the hero Odysseus has secretly returned home incognito to Ithaca after many years away. He is appalled to discover his house inhabited by a group of boorish men known as The Suitors, for in addition to thieving the household food and slaughtering the livestock, these men have been aggressively pursuing Odysseus's wife Penelope, whom they believe to be a widow and are thus hopeful to gain her hand in marriage.

Upon revealing his identity, Odysseus, along with his son Telemachus, mete out a brutal form of private justice. The Suitors are slaughtered by means such as castration and dismemberment. When it is revealed that the twelve female slaves of the household "betrayed" Penelope by coupling with The Suitors, Telemachus gathers the women and,

> "[...] tied the cable of a dark-prowed ship
> to a large pillar, threw one end above the round
> house,

> then pulled it taut and high, so no woman's foot could reach the ground."[3]

This concept of the "fouled" or sullied woman being degraded into something less than human, indeed less than beast, persisted throughout history. An example familiar to most would be the so-called Witch Trials of Salem, Massachusetts in 1692, where some thirteen women were sentenced to hang at that area's Gallows Hill. History has revealed that most, if not all, of the witch craze that seized puritanical segments of American society at that time were rooted more in hysteria than any instances of genuine diablerie.

The same cannot be said, however, of Canada. The True North held no formal witch hunts per se, and while the country had its share of documented trials against witches, most notably in the New France region (now Quebec), the most common punishment resulting from these trials was not death, but banishment from the community. This likely would not have been taken as too great a hardship for the accused *Sorciers*, for many of them already existed on the periphery of townships, living as hermits who kept company of a different sort.

Hanging, and the subsequent ongoing display of the cadaver of the condemned, was not a uniform mode of judicial execution. This process was reserved for certain types of crimes and certain types of criminals. Thieves, as we have seen, would be publicly disgraced in such a

3 *The Odyssey* by Homer.

way, whereas, say, an adulterer or usurer may not have been.

Sometimes this would be a case of the punishment suiting the crime, as in the British process of being Hanged Alive in Chains, where a criminal would not necessarily be granted the mercy of strangulation by rope but would instead be taken to the vicinity of their unlawful action and there be hoisted off the ground by chains. They would then be left to either starve or succumb to the elements, whichever one first delivered the wretch the merciful *coup de grâce*. But even then, their corpse would remain on display for a chosen span of time.

Alternately, "where willful manslaughter is perpetuated, the offender hath his right hand firstly stricken off."[4] The lopping-off of the Hanged One's hand (and the myriad occult processes in which it was later employed) will later be explored in detail.

In fifteenth century Britain, those convicted of piracy would often be submerged in water while bound in chains and left there, usually until three full tides had passed over them. Along the Thames River the bloated, waterlogged corpses would remain in their chains for even longer periods as a deterrent against other seafaring men who may have been harbouring ideas of committing similar crimes.

That these last few examples involve the convicted being returned to the site of their crimes for their actual

4 *Holinshead's Chronicles* by Raphael Holinshead, circa 1586.

execution suggests a belief perhaps more deeply rooted than meting out a punishment befitting of the crime. There is here an emphasis placed on *locality*, one that hints at the notion that sites of violence and/or tragedy become marked. This is the very essence of a classical haunted place, a site where the past is no mere line in a history book but is a lingering echo, a signal waiting for its receptor. The gallows can be seen as an even more profound example of a haunted place, for if crime and punishment both occurred in the same vicinity, the spectral potency is compounded two-fold, leaving an indelible mark on that patch.

Humankind possesses an innate capacity for infinite aspiration as well as the biological tools required to bring many of these aspirations into the realm of the quick as realities, if not physical ones, then certainly conceptual ones; i.e. ideas that take root as wisdom of the folk. How one perceives not just isolated instances of spirit presencing but the concept of Spiritism entire can either enhance or hobble one's interactions with the Otherworld. The philosophy of transcendence is particularly dangerous because it forges an unnecessary level of distinction between the realm of the flesh and the Otherworld of the Dead.

Frequently this stance manifests as the belief that Spirits occupy a realm more refined or higher than the earthly one. From there this cosmology becomes only more elaborate, with notions of celestial afterworlds too lofty to even be conceived of, let alone experienced, by the living. Whatever truth may be drawn from such belief systems is beyond the subject at hand. What is vital to this writing is the concept that magical consciousness is not a skill but a faculty, a Sense by which one perceives not merely the outward form but also the hidden import, the occult significance, the indwelling soul.

One sees that true power is found in the innate, the hidden, the buried. All one requires to perceive is to become properly attuned to their subtle frequencies. What one perceives through the faculty of magical apprehension that I term simply the Poetic Sense is the sublime. And it is sublime in the strictest sense.

Misuse and overuse of the term 'sublime' has lent to it a patina of heavenliness, of elevation. In truth the word refers precisely to experiencing something *beneath the level of the linguistic, logical mind.* Hence, it is sub-liminal, below language, and is either imagistic or non-representational in character. The significance and beauty extant with one's experience of the sublime emanates from what psychologists would term the subconscious. But the form that the sublime chooses to shine through rarely appeals to our rational sense. More often than not, the sublime is touched with some aspect of terror or the uncanny, even the unabashedly hideous. The gallows is equally sublime as it is grotesque. This paradox of the heart is a palpable necessity, for it stretches one's comprehension of that which is sublime. The paradox of simultaneous desire and repulsion tests and broadens us. One's world becomes laden with intimations of the phantasmagorical; hints that gleam, dimly yet unceasingly, like clouded jewels at the hem of one's consciousness.

The gallows and its attendant spirits are neither earthly or celestial in the stricter sense of these terms. They occupy an in-between place and hence they may only be perceived by an in-between awareness. Spirits are seen not with the optic nerves alone, but by the eye infused with the Poetic Sense.

It is this intuitive, receptive faculty that enables one to not only see a given thing but also apprehend and be moved by its invisible, indwelling soul, its significance to the deeper cycles of the universe. This is how the ancient poem can still effectively rouse the modern reader, how the antiquated temple can hoist the spirit of one who crosses its crumbling archway. The wisdom of the elemental world passes through us like the spear that pierces, that traumatizes, the membrane of mundane consciousness and unleashes the fiery blood-wisdom that infuses our lives with the enthusing force of Becoming. When one is in the throes of Becoming, they are neither completed nor have they emptied themselves like the ascetic who strives for the transcendent tranquility of Being.

Becoming is the living surge of the chthonic, the churning of the cauldron. That which is Becoming slithers through the empirical grip, the hand that attempts to capture all phenomena, to contain and name and quantify all in the frantic struggle to keep forms discrete and familiar. In other words, the mind strives vainly to achieve mastery of the wilderness, whose shadows infuse everything, both inside and out. Becoming dashes such rigorous drives. It upsets the familiar and shocks the staid. Becoming is the unbidden surge of erotic fire that immolates the ascetic's trance of material denial. It is the disturbing nightmare that surges up from the sleeper's subconscious.

The Poetic Sense is the robust appreciation of this frustrating paradox, which lies buried in *all* experience. The poet understands that nothing is pure or discrete, that all things carry a trace of their opposer. Love is torturous, and this is part of what makes its bliss so sweet. The Underworld fumes with hellish visions, yet these are the very vessels of the sublime, the masks that lend shape to the ineffable.

That which is Becoming is neither fully matter nor purely image; it is the denizen of the imaginal demimonde that dangles precariously, like the corpse from the gibbet. Authentic apparitions are not merely entopic phenomena, nor do they arise from bough, rope, or soil in and of themselves. Instead the Spiritist who bids solemn entry to the Hanging Place finds themselves within a hinterland where one's worldly wisdom is taxed to its limit, yet the physical form is not made fully manifest.

An example that ably illustrates both the potency of the Hanging Place can be found in Canadian folklore. Here, as is often the wont of magical wisdom, luminous gems of perennial truth are slyly interwoven into the fabric of what is on the surface a simple fireside tale. Such stories usher in a chilly draft of the timeless. Even when precise geographical locales or verifiable historic details are present in a given tale, there is always a degree of separateness from our current perceptions of history, of place. The events that unfurl in folklore occur in a shadowy Double of the familiar world. In this instance, which revolves around the legend of *La Corriveau*, the Quebecois region is reflected in a glass darkly. What we ingest is the land as it is outside of time and before it bore the names and borders we have imposed upon it.

¶

MARIE-JOSEPHTE CORRIVEAU RESIDED in the rural eighteenth century-region of New France. She was the eleventh and only surviving child of a farmer and his wife. In 1763, *La Corriveau*, as she came to be immortalized in folklore, was convicted of mariticide by hatchet and was subsequently sentenced to sixty lashes, branding, and ultimately to the gallows.

It was this, her final punishment, that elevated *La Corriveau* to the mythic status. Once she had been slain by the noose, her lifeless body was ordered to be placed in a gibbet and hung from the limb of a great tree that loomed above a well-trod crossroads near a churchyard. There her remains, scavenged by carrion crows, decayed, wind-lashed, would be witnessed by any who dared traverse by the cemetery. There she became an emblem, a warning of the harsh justice that would befall anyone who dared transgress or transcend the laws of the land. *La Corriveau* became a haunter of her homeland.

One night, a local man unwisely chose to shun his wife's warnings to not pass under *La Corriveau*'s gibbet during the nocturnal hours. She had warned him that although the woman's body had been flensed by time and scavenging birds, *La Corriveau* somehow clung to life. She had also gained the gift of divine sight, for even though her eye-sockets had been picked clean, she was nonetheless able to spot anyone or anything that approached her patch.

Dismissing these claims as pure superstitious foolishness, the man decided to take the notorious crossroads home, as this path was the most direct route to his homestead.

At midnight he reached the gibbet. Mustering his courage, the man ambled down the path by the cemetery. There he could discern, creaking ominously in the night wind, the hanging cage of the creature that had been dubbed New France's 'gallows bird.' Doing his best to avoid so much as an even a lone glance at the tree, the man's heart swelled with fear. He hurried past the churchyard, and immediately upon his passage beneath the Hanging Place his ears were filled with a horrible scraping noise. Terrified, the man stole a quick over-the-shoulder glimpse, and what he saw froze him: the shrill scraping sound was that of *La Corriveau* dragging her gibbeted form along the lonely road. Her fleshless legs dragged uselessly beneath her floating cage. Her skeletal hands were lunging from between the gibbet's bars, reaching and grasping wildly. She pulled her rotted form nearer, nearer...

His mind reeling, the man turned and broke into a frantic run. But his sighting of *La Corriveau* had birthed a profound and overwhelming change in his perception. Turning his focus once more to the road before him, the man noticed a subtle yet undeniable shift in the landscape around him. It had somehow become aroused, woken. The man felt that presences were everywhere. Was this still his homeland?

The trail was luminous with dancing blue flames, ghost-lights that were so vibrant and plentiful the man wondered if all of Canada's damned had flown here for some unknowable purpose.

These ghost-lights then flitted toward the nearby St. Lawrence River, eventually crossing it and congregating on a small island on the far side. Upon this island there stood a hill, and it was to the peak of this hill that the ghost-lights travelled. Once there, they revealed their true form, the one that remained concealed within their glowing vessels.

They were hellish hybrid creatures the likes of which could never be found in the annals of zoology or human history. These monsters formed a great ring at the top of the hill and began to leap, to dance the *Toure-loure*[5] until, at the centre of this grotesque circle, summoned by the mad dancing, the Devil himself appeared. Tall as a church steeple, wearing a tilted cap with a spruce tree for a feather, the Lord of the Sabbath watched with

5 A spiral dance that is a vestigial variant of French Baroque court dances.

his singular eye (a cauldron-hollow socket occupied the space where the other eye should have been) as his devotees danced and howled their praises upon him.

Entranced by this unworldly sight, the man was only faintly aware of the pair of skeletal hands that were gently slipping 'round his throat...until they begin to squeeze.

Seized with panic, the man attempted to wrest himself free, but *La Corriveau* had pulled her gibbeted form onto the man's back. She rasped into his ear that it was her desire to cross the St. Lawrence so that she may join her kin and dance widdershins around her Master on the hill. Being a blessed river, the St. Lawrence was impassable for *La Corriveau* unless she was ferried across it on the back of a good Christian.

The man ardently refused. So, *La Corriveau* warned him that if he would not aid her, she would strangle the life out of him and then fly across the river to the Sabbath mounted upon his damned soul.

Terrified of perdition, the man tried frantically to resist but *La Corriveau* skillfully choked him into unconsciousness. The man eventually awoke, fearing at first that the gallows bird had spirited him away to the Underworld. But the sight of the rising sun and the sound of birdsong reassured him that he was still on Earth. A check of his belongings revealed that *La Corriveau* had drained his brandy flask before returning to her limb above the crossroads. The man hurried home, where he swore an oath to his wife that he would never again venture to the graveyard at night.

The latent truth of fables and folklore (and indeed many religious and spiritual texts) may be yielded by pinpointing their recurrent elements. Words, motifs, or concepts are often repeated as a means of underscoring their import. In the case of this example of ghost-lore, one notes that the absence of one or both eyes results in a deeper visionary faculty. *La Corriveau* is alluded to having almost omniscient abilities despite her head being an eyeless skull. Her master the Devil rises from the hill with only a single eye in his head, yet he is nonetheless able to observe the Sabbatic revelry. Even the mortal man at the heart of this story perceived a marked shift in his surroundings once he passed under the gallows, for the genius loci were roused by his entrance to a forbidden territory and they therefore deemed to become visible to him, first in the form of ghost-lights and later as teratisms upon the Devil's hill.

What links this trio of elements together is the subtextual implication that a) there is a visionary faculty that allows one to perceive with greater acuity than the ordinary consciousness and the five physical senses, and b) presences that are commonly invisible may reveal themselves to witnesses who become seized by this esoteric visionary faculty.

This phenomenon is the radiant opening of the nexus, the immersion into the crux of the Cross where the Otherworld and the material world touch. It is also the cauldron of Becoming that churns hotly at the very point where soul and flesh intersect.

La Corriveau attains spirit-sight after she has been flensed by carrion crows and vultures. The animal kingdom is a multifaceted bastion of sentience and elemental perfection, living channels of esoteric energies. Every beast serves its own unique and vital function within the natural order, and because of this inexorable bond to the deeper, instinctual functioning of the living world, animals have been regarded by myself and others as living totems of esoteric grace and power. Several pantheons, including the Aztec and Egyptian to name but two, have incorporated animals into their divine gods and goddesses, suggesting a reverence and an understanding of the animal kingdom that far surpasses that of those who slaughter beasts as religious appeasements.

Gallows birds are scavengers. Like Anubis, they feast on the dead and carry their fleshly remains away to higher planes. Tibetan sky burials have woven this occurrence into their metaphysical funerary customs for centuries. The crow, too, has its stature in esotericism, seen as a spirit-animal for many; the keeper of secrets, the trickster, the bearer of sorrow or death tidings. They soar patiently above their prey until the appropriate time comes for them to feast.

Upon being devoured, the deceased is reborn, perhaps in another form, or in a different realm. In the case of *La Corriveau*, her remains dangled between the crossroads and the sky, and it was this very precarious internment that gave her power to, on auspicious occasions such as when her terrain was crossed by the living, leave her perch and skulk the earth. The story's protagonist gains his visionary faculty not through diabolic pact, nor even by a thirst for power, but by the breaking of a taboo. In this case, it is his traipsing the churchyard crossroads at night and passing beneath the dreaded gallows that allows the man to bear witness to the revelries of the Spirits that inhabit the Otherworld.

It is worth noting that glimpsing the Realm of the Dead was not the protagonist's intention here. His disregard for the warnings his wife had given him regarding *La Corriveau* was rooted more in his faith in the power of reason rather than a desire to experience a supernatural encounter. He transgresses the Hanging Place simply because it is a more direct route to his home, and yet despite harbouring no intention to taste the reality of the spectres that dwell in that place, the man is given irrefutable proof that hurls him toward an unwavering conviction regarding the reality of spirits and devils. Thus, his experience, while not consciously architected or even bidden by him, nevertheless granted him a certain metaphysical ken.

Crossroads have long acted as nexus points where the hidden grazes the world of discrete forms. The ancient Greeks attributed crossroads to Hecate, the Underworld goddess who was the mistress of sorcery. Her crossroads are the earthy, chthonic byways that the standing cross or crucifix only represents.

As previously noted, the practice of displaying the condemned at the crossroads, which often demarcated the borderland, was widespread throughout history and its grisly presence undoubtedly dissuaded many travelling bandits from practicing their trade in such localities. Yet history also has its accounts of those who, like the man in the tale of *La Corriveau*, did trespass these forbidden grounds under the cover of darkness. Unlike that story's protagonist, however, these transgressors ventured to the gallows for the express purpose of obtaining magical power. An enduring example of this phenomenon is the culling and creation of the Hand of Glory.

European folklore claims that anyone who amputates the hand of one who perished on the gallows shall be afforded various supernatural attributes, such as the ability to enter any building undetected or to disengage any lock. While there is no definitive explanation as to why the Hand of Glory had to be culled from a hanged man, the presence of the gallows in this process is unwaveringly specific. Given this consistency, it is not too great a leap to speculate that the Hand of Glory receives at least some of its power from the Hanging Place itself.

Much of this power is woven into the potency of transgression. The condemned thief, whose actions resulted in his execution and subsequent public displaying of his lifeless remains, had already in life become an Other. He had broken not only the law of the land but also the Commandment that had come down to Moses on Sinai and thus connected Abrahamic civilizations to their celestial monad. To steal is a transgression with not just worldly but metaphysical implications. The thief does not merely offend his fellow mortals, he breaks a cosmic Law in the eyes of those who adhere to the Abrahamic model. The thief's condition is resonant with that of Cain, who became humanity's first Murderer. Both the condemned thief and Cain were cast out. Both were marked, and yet both attained abilities, not despite their fate, but because of it.

While wandering banished through the foreboding wasteland of Nod, it is believed that Cain himself also engaged in thievery. In this desolate place of exile Cain developed cunning, which, despite its seeming kinship to deception, is rooted far more in a kind of rarefied awareness; the emanation from a luminous yet still icily detached echelon of consciousness. It is this Ur-consciousness that enables one to assess every situation, every environ, every encounter so that they may be wrung of any power they might contain.

Cain's connection to the Otherworld is evidenced by the fact that Nod itself was a hinterland. This uncertain terrain was a No Man's Land; a place that was designed neither by nor for human beings. Even today to venture into a No Man's Land is to tempt fate, to abandon the seeming certainties to which we cling so that we may navigate the world around us. To trespass such a place is frightening and perilous, yet it also enables one to "live deliberately," as Henry David Thoreau phrased it. One is tested in such localities, not only physically by the arid and inhospitable topography but also by the magical potency of their genius loci.

The intimations that Nod was an Otherworld survive in modern parlance. To slip, sometimes unwittingly, into slumber is commonly referred to as 'nodding off,' and dream itself is often triangulated as the Land of Nod, an ethereal plane that the dreamer may visit but does not themselves create or conjure. Much like Cain's exile, the magical dreamer may wander Nod but does not permanently dwell there. Cain himself only survived in Nod after he used his skills as the first mason to create for himself and his family the fortified city of Enoch.

But the condemned thief on the gallows finds no such sanctuary. Their Mark is to become an emblem, a warning whose form shrivels and grows livid as it is bullied by the forlorn-sounding winds in the dead of night. The custom of draping the head of the condemned with a hood further transforms them into an object of abjection, for the mask renders the wearer anonymous, unrecognizable to any passersby, including loved ones and friends. Thus, the hanged man is an unwanted Thing, and therefore anyone who would dare to venture toward such an unclean Thing commits a taboo-breaking of their own, and the defilement of the corpse only increases the severity of this.

The taboos of handling the bodies of the dead are myriad and the scope of this stretches beyond the focus of the present work but suffice it to say that since time immemorial the corpse has been viewed as the source of any number of undesirable elements, from disease and uncleanliness to a gateway for unruly spiritual or 'demonic' forces. Therefore, to not only touch but deliberately mutilate a cadaver, especially one who has already been cast as something less than, or Other than, human is an act of almost universal heresy. Add to this the fact that various recipes for the creation of a Hand of Glory require that it is the left or sinistral hand of the thief that be amputated for these purposes and the entire operation becomes saturated with ferocity and fearsomeness enough to dissuade all but the most tenacious of folk.

Petit Albert is something of a catch-all European grimoire, containing folk practices, cabbalistic lore, and magical recipes. It was a popular tome during the early years of the eighteenth century, when pedlars would cart copies from town to town. *Petit Albert* is historically significant if for no other reason than it notoriously details the requirements for the fashioning of a Hand of Glory, as well as listing some of the lesser-known effects of this implement, such as its ability to render a witness awestruck:

> *One takes the right hand or the left of a hanged man exposed on the highways; it is wrapped in a piece of mortuary cloth, in which it is pressed well to make it restore the little blood which might have remained; then put it in an earthen vessel with zimat, saltpetre, salt, and long pepper, all well pulverized: it is left for a fortnight in this pot; then having drawn it, it is exposed to the great sun of the heat, until it has become very dry; and if the sun is not sufficient, it is placed in an oven, which is heated with fern and verbena;*[6] *then*

6 In some regions verbena is known as 'devil's bane' and is also said to have been employed to bathe the wounds of the Christ after his removal from the cross.

> *a kind of candle with hungry fat, virgin wax, and Lapland sisame is composed, and this hand is used with glory as a candlestick, to hold the candle burning; and in all the places where one goes with this fatal instrument, those who remain there remain motionless*"[7]

The Hand was also believed to have been most powerful if amputated during lunar eclipses. As well as its ability to disengage any lock, the Hand of Glory's use as 'dead man's candles' was equally vital to the thief. In addition to the method described in *Petit Albert*, the severed hand could also be treated by encasing it in wax that contained fat from the Hanged Man. Thieves would then ignite several of the fingers as candles and place this guttering creation on the thresholds of the houses they were about to rob. The proximity of the dead man's candles would paralyze the homeowners, seizing them in a catatonic state of Elsewhere trance, making the intruders' task an easy one.

As to the reason why it is called the Hand of Glory, Walter William Skeat, the early twentieth century etymologist, posits that this appellation has its roots in the French term *main de gloire*, which is itself a corruption of the word 'mandragora,' in other words, the mandrake root.[8] This assertion is crucial, for it weds

7 *Secrets merveilleux de la magie naturelle et cabalistique du Petit Albert* by Anonymous. 1752.

8 See *Notes on English Etymology* by William Walter Skeat. Clarendon Press. 1904.

the technology of the Hand of Glory to another of the gallows' most integral magical properties: the alraune, or mandrake root.

Few other botanical specimens are more intimately (though often inaccurately) intertwined with witchcraft and magic than *Mandragora officianarum*. In modern times the employing of plants for the purposes of health or spiritual well-being carries a certain 'Auld Worlde' charm, but of course even the most rudimentary comprehension of history makes it plain that a practical knowledge of the Green Mysteries was, for millennia, a matter not of novelty but necessity. And if one had no personal comprehension of the healing, psychoactive, or dangerous properties of plants, even the sparsest of villages usually had at least one individual who was versed in wortcunning, one whose services could be had for a fee.

Yet even in antiquity, when the drawing forth of a plant's magical properties was far more common and accepted than it is today, mandrake enjoyed a foreboding reputation. The name mandragora is derived from a pair of ancient Greek words that implied 'harmful to cattle,' indicative of the root's toxic properties. It was native to Southern Europe and the Mediterranean, hence the Greek origin of its common name. In the Arabic-speaking regions of the Levant the plant was dubbed 'Satan's Apple' and 'the face of an idol.' These names likely evolved from the combination of both the mandrake's effective properties (both real and imagined) as well as its physical appearance. The root's vaguely humanoid shape implies a graven image, an undeniable creation whose genesis was not by the hand of the Monad.

The plant itself is a brownish root, relatively similar in both look and shape to parsnip. The base of the mandrake typically branches off into two or three root systems that can bore down several feet into the soil where it grows. And it is these forking root systems that lend the root the appearance of a human figure, hence the mandrake's frequent employment as a poppet in many strands of European witchcraft and sorcery.

Idolatry has long been a blasphemy in the Judaic faith due to its contrarian nature against what is believed to be the one true and ineffable father god. Thus, the mandrake root was believed to be malefic in nature. Utter avoidance of it was often advised, though if one were impelled to dig up and utilize the root, they were encouraged to do so in the vicinity of running water in the hope that the nearby current would cleanse the root of its diabolic properties. Further recorded techniques warn against even touching the root, suggesting that one instead clear the area with an iron tool, then tie one end of a rope to the plant and the other as a noose around the neck of a hungry dog, who would then pull out the root. Soon after freeing the alraune, the dog would commonly perish.[9]The tip of the plant, which blooms aboveground, displays both pointed leaves and whitish bellflowers. Whatever fragrance may be exuded

9 *British Library Harley MS 4986*. Anonymous. 12th Century.

by these flowers is overpowered by the foetid scent of the leaves.

As with most plants, mandrake was utilized for various purposes in ancient times. Pliny the Elder (23 CE–79 CE) describes what he believed to be two unique species of mandrake: the male (white mandragora) and the female (black mandragora).[10] This characterization persisted in English folklore, which spoke of both Mandrake and Womandrake.

It is noteworthy that the mandrake possesses poisonous properties, yet it has always been closely associated with the powers of love and Eros. The ancient Hebrews referred to the root as 'dudaim,' meaning 'love apples.' They also believed that the root could turn barren women fertile. Joseph himself was believed to have been conceived after his mother Rachel ingested mandragora.

Aphrodite, goddess of love in ancient Greece, was also known by the alternate title 'Mandragoritis,' meaning 'She of the Mandragora.' Pieces of the root were a common ingredient in love charms, which hopeful suitors carried with them.

In Pliny's era, it was common for physicians to administer a piece of mandrake for their patient to chew on as a form of anaesthetic. As well, the root was frequently employed for its soporific qualities, which were often enhanced by soaking the mandrake in wine prior to administration.

10 See *Natural History* by Pliny the Elder. (Various editions).

Sleep and the gallows' root are intimately intertwined. The plant is a floral Oneiroi that sweeps the user across the threshold of waking consciousness into Dream or the death-like slumber known in Sanskrit as *sushupti* ('dreamless sleep').

Mandrake was also prescribed to those who were suffering from what were believed to be spiritual afflictions, specifically, demonic possession. Apuleius, for instance, offers the following prescription:

> For witlessness, that is devil sickness or demoniacal possession, take from the body of this said wort mandrake by the weight of three pennies, administer to drink in warm water as he may find most convenient—soon he will be healed.[11]

The effectiveness of mandrake in the banishing of demons is later reinforced by the Romano-Jewish scholar, Flavius Josephus, who, in his *The Wars of the Jews, or, The History of the Destruction of Jerusalem* (78 CE), paints a vivid picture of not only its exorcising powers, but also the fearful, perilous nature of the plant and its environ. Here, the root grew in a region known as Baaras, a name by which the mandrake root was also known in Jerusalem. Josephus describes the following:

> [...] a certain place called Baaras, which produces a root of the same name with itself its color is like to

11 *The Herbarium of Apuleius*, circa 400 CE.

> that of flame, and towards the evenings it sends out a certain ray like lightning.[12]

Josephus goes on throughout this section of his work to imply that the mandrake's strange potencies can be traced, to a certain degree at least, to the foreboding environ in which it bloomed; in this instance, is the land of Baraas, which the author describes as a place of an uncertain and unsettling character. This chimes with innumerable descriptions of the Hanging Place.

Given the abundant accounts that attest to the mandrake's restorative properties and its ability to spiritually cleanse, it is quite plain that the root was equally fey as it was diabolical in its essential makeup. To wit, the following description, found in a twelfth century manuscript:

> It shines at night like a lamp, and when you see it mark it round quickly with iron lest it escape you. For so strong is this power in it, that if it sees an unclean man coming to it, it runs away.[13]

The root's luminous quality is likely a result of its flesh assuming a bluish tinge whenever the evening dew that had collected on its leaves was brightened by moon-

12 *The History of the Jewish War against the Romans* by Flavius Josephus (78 CE).*Book VII*, Chapter 6, Section III. 78 CE. (Various editions.)

13 *The British Library Harley Manuscript 4986*. Circa 12th Century. George C. Druce (translator). 1919.

light. Nevertheless, this optical effect is but one of the traits that enhanced the ancient suspicions about the mandrake's liminality. There was a belief that the mandrake grew simply in the East, near Paradise. East is the compass point of horizon, the hem where clay and stars touch. This is the geographic representation of the gate between states of being, such as waking and dreaming, as well as the nexus of soul and skin, which is the throne of supreme reality, for it is matter fully infused with its own innermost meaning, and the innermost meaning granted full expression in the outer realm. This is true *galgon,* the two poles of the authentic Hanging Place.

The Song of Solomon also hints at the mandragora being indigenous to portals, or more specifically, gates:

> The mandrakes give a smell, and at our gates are all manner of pleasant fruits, new and old, which I have laid up for thee, O my beloved.[14]

In his wryly-titled book *Vera Historia,* Lucian, the 2nd century satirist and proto-fantasist, describes the city of Sleep as being surrounded by a wood in which the trees are tall poppies and mandragoras, with a multitude of bats perched on the limbs.[15]

John Donne, the metaphysical poet, underscored the Edenic origins of the mandragora in his pneumatology

14 Song of Solomon 7:13. KJV.

15 *A True Story* by Lucian of Samosata. A. M. Harmon (transl.). New York, G.P. Putnam's Sons. (1913).

treatise *Infinitati Sacrum* (or alternately, *Metempsychosis*). Here, Donne draws a direct parallel between the organic shape of the mandrake and that of the crucified god:

> His right arme he thrust out towards the East,
> West-ward his left; th'ends did themselves digest
> Into ten lesser strings, these fingers were:
> And as a slumberer stretching on his bed...[16]

Here, too, the fidelity between the realm of slumber and the mandragora is shown.

The mandrake exudes a significance greater than its strange appearance, its physical presence. It is the fruit of Elsewhere, the rare apple whose flesh offers the forbidden knowledge that gave the alpha woman and man the level of detachment necessary for the poetical apprehension of who and where they were. The first Lovers became aware of Eden by the eating of the Devil's Apple, by being banished and no longer a part of paradise. Instead they came to see it for what it was, without falsehood or deception. While this knowledge is often cast in a punitive light, it was in fact a liberation, for the poison fruit of Eden afforded the eater the solitude of soul and silence of spirit to avoid being swept up in the tides of emotional immersion that comes when one is of a place, rather than being of Elsewhere. As Donne phrased it,

16 *Metempsychosis*: *Poêma Satyricon* by John Donne. Verse XV. (1602).

The plant thus abled, to it selfe did force
A place, where no place was; by natures course[17]

The implication here is that the properties of mandragora stretch one's perceptions of time and space. Such an implication has also been expounded by modern authors of plant arcana, who refer to the mandragora and its kin as 'chronophagoi' ('time-eaters')[18]. In this respect, the mandrake is linked to Saturn, whose ravening jaws devour all living things into the timeless void of death. Ingestion of chronophagoi forges, both subjectively and on the physical plane, a liminality, a place where no place was. This sacred clearing is made manifest via poisoning. This can be achieved only when a precise symbiosis has been reached between the visitant who stands in the present and the Spirits of Place whose habitat is the concealed plane of shadows and astral shimmer; a timeless (in the true sense of the word, for it is without time) realm that we often perceive as the ancient past, but is in truth vitality present at the very hem of our awareness at any given moment.

All that remains there in this Otherworld is the quintessence of all beings, all sentient things, human and non-human alike. This plane is the dwelling of the *Fylgjur* or Fetches. It is these Spirit-Doubles, whose mirror-forms are our own flesh-and-blood bodies, that

17 Ibid. Verse XIV.

18 See 'Book of the Skull Orchard' in *Viridarium Umbris* by Daniel A. Schulke. Xoanon, 2005, page 490.

enable the living to perceive through the Moribund Portal, to experience Spectral Resonance, and to enjoy the interpenetration of the realm of the Dead and this, the land of the quick.

One's personal *Fylgja* is the cord that binds their outer vessel to their deepest roots of *Wyrd,* of Fate. Our *Fylgja* is our one true Teacher, the ethereal potency that gives us faculty to even perceive the Otherworld in the first place.

Heed well your own Shade from the Otherworld, for to ignore or dishonour one's own *Wyrd* is to lose all connection to not only one's roots (or soul), but also to their own opportunity at a full and meaningful existence here on Earth.

Your *Fylgja* finds expression and exercise in your own Becoming, the fluidic liberation of shapeshifting and rarefied states of consciousness. Deny it these arenas of expression and you may find your Double creeping autonomously through the waking world. History and folklore are filled with endless accounts of people's *Fylgja* being seen by others, or worse still, by the person themselves. To see one's *Fylgja* in waking life is an ominous portent, a sign that one may be well on their way to permanently crossing through the Veil.

Technology and other baubles of civilization are soulless things and therefore cannot withstand the transition that occurs via trance, vision, or rarefying death. The only caveat to this would be the human-wrought fetishes and primal works that are visceral extensions of the artist's hand and eye. These serve as portals to subtler states of awareness. Creations such as these, although they did not originate in Nature, do have a spectral reflex, a shadow, in the Otherworld. This is so because the fashioning of such genuinely outré or oneiric works were inspired by their creator's original apprehension of the Otherworld. That the artist, the sorcerer, or the dreamer can draw creative inspiration from their glimpses into the sphere of the Dead and the gods reveals a highly important principle that distinguishes this realm from other more purely transcendental spiritual planes, such as Heaven or Nirvana.

This Otherworld *maintains its ties to the causal world of the present that is occupied by the living*. Furthermore, this realm may be interpenetrated; Spirits slip into the quick, and the quick peer into the Spirit realm, all according to the nature of one's bond with their *Fylgja*. Signs and portals of this Otherworld are all around us, but because such clues are either incredibly subtle (i.e. the portent 'happened upon' in Nature, the cherished heirloom that somehow allows the one who bequeathed it to be almost instantly present, the forlorn place that feeds the visitor a true sense of homecoming) or incredibly alien (i.e. the magical dream, the inexplicable fear one may feel toward a certain old house or ruin, etcetera) many who might encounter them are likely to either reject, misconstrue, or simply remain oblivious to them.

Earlier it was detailed how the rarefied aura of the mandrake root has its ties to the Hand of Glory, but its marriage to the gallows runs even deeper than this linguistic or semiotic connection.

J. G. Frazer points out that in Germany the connection between the gallows and the mandrake was so thorough that the root came to bear the name 'Little Gallows Man,'[19] for it was there that the grisly legend of the mandrake being spawned by the spilt seed of a hanged man (or more precisely, a hanged thief) began. The potency of bodily fluids, especially blood and semen, have been demonstrated in various magical, alchemical and Tantric traditions, and the uses to which these fluids may be applied are legion. The mandragora, or alraune, is a life-form, a mannikin infused with some form of consciousness, rather than an inert poppet whose life and utility is dependent upon the cunning and capabilities of its crafter.

To retrieve the alraune, one was advised to venture to the gallows after sunset on a Friday, with their ears plugged with pitch or wax to avoid hearing the fatal shriek that the root would emit upon being disinterred.

Friday is the domain of Freyja, the Norse goddess of fertility, love, sex, wealth and death. It is fitting, then, that the Germanic tradition urges one to undertake a pilgrimage to the gallows on Her day, for there is a definite element of impersonal lust inherent in the fallen seed of the condemned.[20]

19 See *Jacob and the Mandrakes* by J. G. Frazer. Oxford University Press. 1917.

20 The French poet Tristan Corbière wrote of his yearning "To come like a hanged man."

This form of ejaculation has its basis in physical reality: when the carotid arteries and jugular vein are constricted by the noose, blood may rush to the phallus. This, combined with the convulsive motions of struggle and death throes, can result in spontaneous erection and ejaculation.

Consider the mystical ramifications of having one's life extinguished by forbidding air to pass through the throat, which has been constricted by the noose. As the rope robs the condemned of breath, there is an invisible cleaving, a separation, a distinction not only of the living from the dead, but between the condemned and the very cosmic essence of life. Hinduism teaches that *prana* is the very essence of consciousness. So fundamental is its role in the universe, one requires no understanding of its essential nature for one to both access it and receive its boons, for *prana* is said to reach all sentient beings through breath itself, entering us and infusing us not only with vitality but with the capacity to understand and revel in this vitality. To forbid one this sacred breath is to hurl them into something outside of the cosmic continuum. The corpse has served as not only an host of unclean and afflicted powers: disease, rot, et cetera. Yet it has also long been believed to be a repository of magical properties that can only be accessed by some form of contact with the corpse itself.

The practice of preserving and tending to the remains of the dead to achieve some level of communion and resonance with the spirit realm, even if that spirit realm was restricted to ensuring that the deceased be remembered, that their deeds and character not be cast off into the mists of history, was practically universal.

Ossuaries and holy reliquaries persist as examples of this. *Memento Mori* was not the sole use of these death relics. For just as the diabolist of the past would have employed the Hand of Glory in their craft, priests would raise the preserved hands of dead holy men, such as Saint Stephen, to bless their congregation. These grisly relics were commonly preserved in lavish cases or cabinets that functioned to both protect the specimen while at the same time reverencing its sacredness.

Being in the presence of such artifacts provides a potently direct form of Gnosis that can only come through visceral experience—proximity to remains, silent and solitary observation in charnel houses or cemeteries, the earnest, selfless call to the Otherworld and the receptiveness toward the delicate traces of Spirit response—and not the mere simulacrum or imagined scenarios that can be had by remaining inside one's cloistered chamber.

Proximity to morbidity and decay does not merely represent death but in fact becomes the very seam that the living believe distinguishes them from the Dead. An inscription that can be found in a Maltese chapel of bones communicates this notion succinctly: "Death breaks and dissolves the illusion and is the boundary of all mortal things."

History has its examples of those who have forcefully breached this boundary, some with acts that illustrate the connection between the extinguishing of *prana* by strangulation as an act of sacrifice. The Thuggee of India were a notorious band of highwaymen and murderers who reportedly fancied themselves to be the spawn of the sweat of Kali-ma, the Hindu goddess of destruction whose essence imbues this, the Iron Age of Darkness. Thuggee members would insinuate themselves into travelling parties before luring individual members to places of seclusion. There, the unsuspecting victim would be garroted in a silent, meticulous manner. The dying were believed to have had their limbs bent into particular *asanas* in the hope that they would be seen as worthy sacrifices to Kali, blood-sustenance to feed the Mother of Darkness.

By these sacrifices, the Thuggee may have understood the mystical implications that the extermination of breath would have, not only to the physical form but also their victim's *suksma sarira* (subtle body).

What is cinched within the noose is Vishudha, the fifth primary chakra, whose domain in the human body is the pit of the throat. The literature of many schools of Eastern tradition all concur that the appearance of this etheric presence is like that of a full moon framed by smoke petals of purple. This is of course suggestive of lunar power, which the human organism interprets via receptivity, a certain cold, fey aloofness, and receives through the vital phenomena of dreams and visions.

Vishuddha's function is that of purification. Yet it must be stressed that this term is not here used in any moralistic sense. This mode of purification has no relation to refining the 'good' from the 'bad.' Dualisms such as this do not apply. The purification here might be more accurately described as a mode of discernment, for what is being separated or distinguished here are powers and poisons.

The throat chakra is the receptacle of *amrita*, the sacred nectar that drips down from the realm of the gods to the human organism. *Amrita* is akin to the Greek concept of ambrosia, as well as that of ichor; the sidereal property of the blood of the gods. It also connects to the blasphemous Wine of the Witches' Sabbath, particularly the Sabbath as it was conveyed in the works of occultists such as Austin Osman Spare and Andrew D. Chumbley.

What links these examples, more of which can be yielded by the interested student who pursues the subject on their own, is that the sacred fluid emanates from a higher or more rarefied plane and that its sacred properties may be bestowed upon the worthy aspirant, thereby granting them the experience of the Otherworld while the aspirant himself remains enfleshed. Said experience may issue forth as a full understanding of past and present.

By comprehending these vast cycles of time, there is an unspoken implication that the experiencer must somehow be removed from time itself. The touch of the timeless is often alarmingly fresh, leading one to see just how unaware their psyche had been, how automatically they had been functioning until that lightning flash instant of self-awareness alerted them to who and where they were, and what they are Becoming. Austin Spare defined this state of mystical liberation as Kia, the otherwise nameless fiery radiance that is neither potential nor manifestation, but is a fluidic in-between-ness, a liminal state of ecstasy. Within this timeless freedom, Becoming is experienced as scintillating, immediate reality. ("Time has not changed it, hence I call it new."[21])

This timeless realm from which *Amrita* (or Kia) flows alters the temporal realm. One is not granted entry into the plane of the gods, nor do the gods themselves assume the flesh and form of the physical plane. What occurs instead is a symbiosis, the harmonic chiming between Spirit and skin; i.e. Spectral Resonance.

The Vishuddha chakra is particularly connected to dream. The Vajrayana tradition of Buddhism emphasizes this and advises regular meditation upon the throat chakra can lead to spiritual experiences by way of lucid dreaming.

There exists a rare and rarefied form of dreaming that functions as a point of rendezvous between the dreamer and the Dead. By 'the Dead' I am not referring exclusively to the ghosts of deceased humans, though such presences are unquestionably endemic to this form of dream. Non-human spirits also occupy such realms and what's more, their ability to communicate and/or interact with one's dreaming self may be equally impactful and vital as the messages of the human spirit. I here use 'the Dead' as an umbrella term to encompass both humans who are disincarnated as well as those presences

21 *The Book of Pleasure (Self Love): The Psychology of Ecstasy* by Austin Osman Spare.

which may have never manifested in any tangible form in the waking world, save for fleeting apparitions or eerie impressions. As to why I correlate the two, my reasoning springs from direct encounter during magical dreams, whereupon tutelary spirits have conveyed, through gesture, symbol, and utterance alike, that one's very nature becomes profoundly altered the longer they dwell in the Otherworld. This symbiosis can often manifest as dream. This I can attest to, for the present work only came to be after, unbidden, its essential nature was presented to me by the numen of the gallows via dream.

Dream has ushered me into the Halls occupied by the ghosts of those I knew well in life, individuals who exhibited no noticeable traits of sorcerous knowledge or magical skill while they were incarnate, and yet their passage across the river Styx to the realm of the Dead has blessed them with a wisdom and a ken for the Art that we know as sorcery or witchcraft that transcends anything I have ever witnessed by even the most learned and seasoned of living practitioners. This is so because what endures to reach the far bank of the Styx is one's quintessence, their *Fylgja*. Regardless of whether a person "believed in" or participated in Spiritist activity in life, their *Fylgja* can adapt and flourish with shocking adeptness once the chains of egoic hubris have been immolated in the furnace of death.

The tenure of the deceased in the Otherworld is what has infused their subtle, disincarnated form with these talents. There, the barrier of matter and cause-and-effect reasoning has dissolved, making the human and the unhuman kin. There, one's knowledge and experience of the primordial suffers no dilution through the flaws, whims, and worries of a human teacher. Instead there is a kind of direct transfusion. One becomes the Other, and that which once comprised their personality dissolves like soaked sugar. What endures is not one's 'True Self,' at least not in the sense of the willed creation that the living cling to in the hope of wielding conscious mastery over all that they survey. It may well be that one's *Fylgja* will be utterly alien to what a person seemed in life. Such is the Mystery of contagion, of the wisdom of poisoning.

As to how dream enables one incarnate to traverse to the Otherworld, the root lies in the agility of the *Fylgja,* which, as our ancestors knew only too well, possesses the capability to depart the body and move about without being tethered to the human computer that relies upon the filtering faculty of the five physical senses. The spirit that might have, in waking life, manifested as an uncanny feeling or flitting form in one's periphery can be met directly and interacted with in the rarefied state of the magical dream.

How might the dreaming self relate to the gallows? When the throat is cinched, *those discerning abilities that allowed the subtle body to distinguish power from poison become mangled.* The result is that one's powers become poisonous, and the blighted in turn become holy. This is the nature of nocturnal Gnosis, for which transgression, peril, and the awe-ful are adamantine requisites.

One must pay the worldly tariff if they wish to taste the ambrosial blood of the gods.

The Hindu deity of this throat region is Ambara, a white, four-armed figure who sits atop a white elephant. Resplendent as silvery moonlight, Ambara, like many Hindu deities, carries with him both boons and agonies, which, absorbed in proper measure, result in liberation.

I would be remiss were I not to single out the fact that one of the items that Ambara carries in his quartet of hands is none other than the noose.

FOR ALL THE layers of meaning we have explored in relation to the Hanging Place, there is perhaps even more significance to be found in the figure of the Hanged One itself.

As was illustrated earlier with the tale of *La Corriveau*, there is a certain rarefication of self that occurs after one has been condemned by others to hang. But this rarefication has little connection to punishment, or indeed any of the laws of humanity. It has more to do with the myriad implications that become palpably presenced in the figure of the One Who Hangs. For they have, against all reason, become the occupant of that thin, fleeting in-between-ness, the plane that is neither terrestrial nor empyrean, the phantasmagorical demimonde from which is drawn all our tales of Gothic horror, through which we make pilgrimage while in the throes of our darkest nightmares.

The One Who Hangs is no longer earthbound. Their feet do not tread the clay of the terra firma. But neither do they show signs of transcendence or transmutation. They remain between the elements of earth and air, their body—breathing or utterly lifeless, it makes no difference—on full display, an undignified object of abjection. Indeed, the abject feels somehow not a part of our world and instead some unseemly interloper from elsewhere, from an Otherworld. As an emblem, the One Who Hangs is not merely deceased, they are occupants of that thin space that is free of earthly tethers and yet, because their noose tethers them to the loftier eyrie of this plane, they may still observe this world from a rarefied perspective.

The Hanged Man, the twelfth Trump card of Tarot's Major Arcana is a layered example of this concept. The Hanged Man's central image is of a nameless (and sometimes faceless) figure dangling upside down, his foot or ankle affixed to a tree or a pillar. In addition to this core figure, different Tarot decks adorn The Hanged Man with symbols or 'clues' that align it to whichever tradition or bent a given deck may have as its focus. It is common to see his legs clad in red, symbolizing fire, while his shirt is blue, indicating his representation of the element of water, for The Hanged Man is a receptive principle. He is willing to maim and reposition his body on the tree of the world to better attune himself to the subtle Gnosis of the Otherworld, which in the outer world is disguised as untamed Nature and into the psychophysical complex of humanity is known as the depths of the subconscious.

As the twelfth card, The Hanged Man numerically represents a completed cycle, be it the twelve months of the calendar or the twelve signs of the zodiac. More pointedly, The Hanged Man represents *manifestation*, the point at which one's depth experience undergoes translation into some notable, vouch-worthy expression that makes plain to those with eyes to see that one has obtained hard-won experiential wisdom, a secret that now infuses their entire being.

The cross upon which this figure is hanged is the Tau Cross, which symbolizes totality, the Mysteries entire. The Hanged Man is sacrificed, but this is not an act of salvation undertaken to usher others into a promised land. Rather it is the sacrifice of self unto self. What is offered as sacrifice is the egoic construct of the personality and all that this encompasses, such as want, desires for an ideal future, the attempt to divert one's Wyrd in favour of a small segment of personal 'victory' over life's obstacles.

The distinction must here be made between Wyrd and determinism.

Wyrd must not be equated with fate as it is commonly understood, namely the inexorable and inescapable lot that has been cast for one's life. Wyrd is the primordial and impersonal quintessence that transcends the personality and is also apart from natural law.

At the bottom of the Well of Urd, the divine Norns have carved the nascent destinies of all living things into the roots of the *Yggdrassil*, yet Wyrd can be also be shaped. It is not an ironclad or inexorable. It is nevertheless a curse to those who choose to live in self-delusion or ignorance of their innermost nature, their *Fylgja*. Such people will never know the blessings of Wyrd or experience the divinity of the realm of gods and spirits.

Those who actively strive to experience and express their innermost nature, who become the artist, the blacksmith, the seer; the one who acknowledges the presence of the hidden presences here in Midgard; their lives shall be infused with the deepest powers of their primordial Wyrd. Their roots shall be nourished and the limbs of their deeds and words will reach far. To partake of Wyrd is to experience a quickening of the soul.

It was this form of esoteric wisdom that Odin sought and was willing to offer himself in the hope of obtaining.

To sacrifice one's egoic personality is not to simply submit and bow one's head to the whims of natural law. This form of self-sacrifice is a broadening of one's Circle. Becoming, as opposed to the eviscerated transcendentalist aloofness of being, involves the presencing of one's world with those powers that reverence for the personality obscures, if not stifles altogether. Wyrd is the turning of the wheel. It is manifestation, that which happens, or more precisely, that which happens through vast cycles of which one may gain awareness by their own initiatory endeavours.

Water is the element of The Hanged Man, the element of receptivity, the untamed roil of the subconscious, of intuition. Water is a feminine principle. It is a chthonic power, the womb of the Black Mother whose fathoms dwell in each of us as our unfathomable impulses, the unbearable drives and visions that erupt from our subconscious. The retinue of the shadow-laden strata come alive via the Art. These forms can never be apprehended fully, but only intimated through dream, through intuition, and in the throes of Eros and creativity.

The Hanged Man, being inverse, is diving headlong into this Well of Mysteries, the uncontrollable chthonic cauldron. It is this pose that informs the common equation of the figure of the Hanged Man with the Norse god Odin.

Odin willingly sacrificed himself in the hope of gaining arcane knowledge. This example is significant because it evidences the fact that the Hanged One is not necessarily the condemned one. There are those whose thirst for the Hidden is so great that they lay body and well-being upon the altar of sacrifice. They self-torture with the knowledge that sacrifice entails pain, hardship, testing, but they also sacrifice with the knowledge that a thing is made sacred by such unpleasant and trying elements. Odin has long been one of the preeminent models of this principle.

In Norse lore, Odin ventured to the *Yggdrasil*, the Ash Tree that towered as the spine of the world. The roots of *Yggdrasil* are nourished by the Well of Urd, the repository of the past, of the Dreamtime. *Yggdrasil* is manifested in the present moment, the now. The interconnection between these two vistas of time is the very crux of Spectral Resonance; the reconfiguration of one's own orientation in relation to place and time.

Yggdrassil was the material medium through which Odin could draw power from the ancient past, whose essence was housed in the Well of Urd. Odin was wise enough to understand that he could not draw from the Well in the same manner as the Tree itself, which culled nourishment into its very roots. For him to access those same depths, drastic and altogether different measures were required.

Thus, Odin hung himself upside down from a gnarled bough so that he might perceive the Below. There he remained, disoriented and anguished, for nine nights. By this self-sacrifice and incalculable tenacity, Odin proved his worth. In matters of spirit-pacts, there is perhaps no principle of grander importance than sincerity of intent. The road to Hell is paved with good intentions, as the old axiom goes, but it should be clarified that sincerity and goodness are not inherently synonymous. One may harbour noble intentions, but the entertaining of ideas, opinions or philosophies alone has no currency in the Otherworld. Manifestation of one's intent is the requisite for forging a spirit-pact.

Such expressions should be considered carefully, for the aspirant should ensure that the manifestation of their intentions involves appropriate tone of gesture and speech (if any utterances are made, and these need not be linguistic), correct implements, and most importantly, a suitable sacrifice.

The very concept of sacrifice is a complex and controversial topic. While the dramatic images of animal or human extermination are most commonly drudged up when the topic is broached, sacrifice, *genuine* sacrifice, is not about mere bloodletting or carnage. It is about penetrating or afflicting the manifest form to stimulate or reveal its hidden inner significance, its soul, thereby sacralising it. Such a thing can be achieved by earnest meditation upon the fetish or the painting so that its inspiring genius might be communicated, or through the respectful observation or mimicry of the beasts in the wild, or indeed by the putting of one's *own* body through pain or discomfort to arouse the poetic sense that is Becoming.

It may well be that an individual is more prone to place another being on the sacrificial altar simply because they are not willing to put themselves through any true hardship. They prefer the edgy glamour of occultism to the challenges and hardships of authentic initiation.

While sacrifice need not necessarily involve bloodletting or loss of life, initiatory actions must nevertheless be taxing. Odin hung himself between soil and sky, denying himself sleep or nourishment. This he did to express his sincerity of intent. To simply yearn for hidden knowledge or depth experiences is pure whimsy that leads nowhere. Worse than the errant wish for such forms of experience is the endemic of modern thought, namely that one is simply entitled to such experiences.

In the realms of the hidden and the esoteric, there is neither democracy nor diplomacy. While this fact may not hew with many aspects of contemporary culture (western culture in particular), it must be stated that initiation is not for all, even if one possesses or feels they possess an innate draw toward spiritual or metaphysical matters. The most primary steps into the traditions of spiritist or esoteric endeavour will reveal not egalitarianism, but hierarchy. Whether exploring the contemporary fraternal or sororal Lodge, the agrarian witches' coven, or researching the priesthoods of ancient Pharaonic Egypt, one quickly learns that an initiate either earns one's place or they suffer the pains and failures of disingenuousness.

The teachings of true sodalities are justly guarded and are doled out piecemeal, according to the dedication, tenure, and worth of the novitiate. One must question any sodality that exudes a homey emotive air, or that ascribes blatantly human motivations to whatever gods, goddesses, or spirits they claim to be working with. Such an atmosphere suggests a secular club designed to bolster its members' sense of self-worth or their sense of belonging.

Conversely, one *should* look for, even seek out, a certain caginess on the part of their chosen sodality. One should absolutely be tested and vetted before any deeper teachings are imparted. For just as a student may harbour wariness toward a potential teacher, a teacher should also demonstrate caution and an austerity befitting of the Gnosis they have obtained.

An apt example of this can be found in an Eighth Century legend of the Visigoth kings, who were said to have erected a Tower of Secrets that was secured by multiple locks. Upon the royal election (for Visigothic monarchs were coronated by way of clan votes based on their character and deeds rather than the more conventional mode of monarchal bloodlines), the newly appointed king would be furnished with a new lock and then duly led to the Tower of Secrets. There, he would swear an oath to never even discover (let alone disclose) whatever Mysteries were contained within the Tower. His charge as king as not to learn the secrets, but to guard them, to preserve their sacred Mystery. The king's lock would then be added to the multiple others, the latest in a succession of safeguards that symbolized the value the kings placed on maintaining the Tower's Secrets.

The principle behind this legend is one that much of the contemporary occult field can benefit from; namely that the true value of esotericism lies not in the answers it might provide but in the ambience and numinous power that radiates from Mystery itself.

Too often individuals approach initiation as a kind of *avant garde* game, an intellectual riddle that can be cracked by absorbing and regurgitating a glut of arcane data. Nothing could be further from the truth. (For an example of just how disastrous this lust for arcane knowledge can be, seek out the legend of the fate of

Saint Roderick in connection to the Visigoth Tower of Secrets[22].)

Those who have touched or been touched by the authentic, who have stood in the presence of gods and spirits, come away not just changed, but *afflicted* by these experiences. The true esotericist bears a kind of invisible but perceivable Mark as surely as Cain did when he breached cosmic law and nodded off in that arid wasteland of blood, soil, and lunar Otherness.

Gnosis can be experienced by simpleton or scholar alike. Intelligence might provide these Gnostic flashes with context or a more nuanced comprehension of their underpinnings, but intelligence alone is no guarantor of access to the Mysteries. This fact is compounded when said intelligence is only fed by text and is never physically manifested or tested in the wilderness of the True. Know well that while we are here exploring and expounding upon the nature of the Otherworld of Spirits, there is a paradox that is inextricably woven into the fabric of such endeavours: the Otherworld cannot be equated with any sort of empyrean kingdom, nor can the interpenetration of waking and dream, of the incarnate and the spectral, be accurately described as transcendentalist.

Devotional practices such as ascetism (where the sensorial realm is shunned so that one may strive to access a higher strata of consciousness) has its place in

22 See *Mysteries of the Goths* by Edred Thorsson. Runa-Raven Press. 2007.

the long and multifaceted realm of magic, mysticism and religion, but it is decidedly not akin to Spiritism, or to sorcery. In this Art, the flesh and the realm of the senses play a pivotal, if paradoxical, role.

There are certain spirits who crave, or simply enjoy, the 'use' of a living Initiate. One need look no further than the traditions of Voudon, where Mambos and Houngans may be 'ridden' by foreign spirits or gods, their bodies becoming as horses for these powers, which Maya Deren notably referred to as the Divine Horsemen. Beyond this, there are unquantifiable examples of seers, artists, witches, shamans, mediums and scryers who have lent themselves to visitant spirits in exchange for visions, knowledge and sensual awareness of the Otherworld. Such relationships must be fostered with offerings and adherence, and the fruits of these interactions may not necessarily manifest as blessings.

The more one keeps company with Otherness, the more Other one becomes.

One's interpenetration of the Otherworld will alter the entirety of their being; how they reckon time, the rhythm of their daily routine, the way in which they determine the treasure from the dross. All these things and more will be tainted so that they become evermore attuned to the ways of the Otherworld. This alteration is an unmistakable hallmark of Spectral Resonance, recognizable to all who walk such paths.

Another way that the flesh may be employed to spawn such a relationship is to test its limits. Humanity often defines the sensorial realm and the flesh as arenas of pleasure, of carnal indulgence, which undeniably have their place in life, but if one desires to glimpse through the Moribund Portal, to perceive that realm where the flesh is forbidden, a tariff must be paid. At times this may be something as simple as laying out a coin of the realm as admission so that one may be ferried via trance across the Styx. At other times, the price will be much dearer, requiring more extreme measures.

Odin's motivation for hanging inverse upon the *Yggdrassil* was a desire for knowledge. While this is accurate in a broader sense, the knowledge sought by Odin was not mere information, for the apprehension of such information, especially today, where information is ubiquitous to the point of becoming nearly worthless because it lacks context and nuance, offers no enhancement to one's Becoming. The knowledge Odin sought was experiential, deep. It flowed from the powers of Urd, the essence of timelessness.

What erupted from the depths to reach Odin on that ninth night was not the 'divine' Word, but the occult symbol-set of the runes, which Odin then carried back to Midgard and imparted to his people. He returned not with a set of didactic laws, but a magical grammar, a grimoire of vital symbols that could unseal the deeps of one's consciousness, both through meditation upon them and active Work with them.

Contrast this with Moses, whose received transmission was thoroughly transcendental in nature. Moses ascended a mountain to be nearer to the unseen monad whose kingdom cannot be truly apprehended until after one's body has perished. What Moses returned with were commandments, edicts to which one had to adhere on faith alone if one wished to experience some future Promised Land.

Odin climbed no mountain. His journey was not to an arid peak. He oriented himself in a jarringly unorthodox fashion; suspending himself inversely. His positioning alone would be viewed as heretical when measured against the accepted mores of decency. In Renaissance-era Italy, ignoble individuals such as thieves (see earlier discussion in this book) would be subject to public humiliation by a *pittura infamante* a 'defaming portrait' that always showed the condemned as hanging upside down by their ankle, symbolizing their humiliation against societal laws and the customs of righteousness. (Art historians concur that the *pittura infamante* led to the common image of the Hanged Man card in Tarot.)

Odin drew his power not from a lofty mountaintop, but from a shadow-drenched Well, from the subterranean. His was a chthonic, rather than a celestial, power. What arose from the Well of Urd were not edicts, but Gateways. The runes are the very essence of the Mysteries; glyphs whose angles are found nowhere in nature, thus, their very form carries an intimation of elsewhere. Their meaning cannot be gleaned by examining their shape alone. Instead each rune must be ingested, so to speak, so that it can incubate in a person's soul, where its esoteric value may be felt after it has hatched like a seed and its roots have bored down into one's subconscious. This is the womb of the Dark Mother, the cauldron of submerged forces that surge autonomously, beyond the reach of the conscious Apollonian mind.

A knowing eye can discern runic shapes in the structural beams of a typical gallows the design of at least two runes; specifically, the Algiz (ᛉ) and Wunjo (ᚹ) runes.

Such apprehensions might be dismissed out of hand as nothing more than an instance of what psychology terms pareidolia—a psychophysical phenomenon whereby the brain reflexively hunts for and hastily forms familiar, even profound, patterns from what is in objective reality a mere jumble of random data—it has become an all-too-human impulse to weigh any and all experiences upon the scale of the physical sciences, or worse still, upon theories that carry with them merely the convenient air of the seemingly logical and utilitarian.

Setting aside the benefits that scientific inquiry has brought to humanity, it must be stressed that many of the discoveries and methods of science have been in existence for millennia. Furthermore, science was never designed to serve as the catch-all method that could 'solve' (and thereby conquer) every aspect of existence. It is only in this, the technology-addicted, humancentric modern age, that has truly inflated science to this lofty height and it has come to be regarded by many with, ironically enough, a kind of religious zealotry.

The esotericist appreciates that while science is an immensely effective tool for studying and cataloguing the realm of matter, this same effectiveness simply does not apply when exploring the subtle realms of consciousness and immateriality. The reason for this is because such phenomena is truly the ghost in the machine; the soul which infuses awareness, indeed is awareness itself. As philosopher Alan Watts remarked, "Nothing so eludes conscious inspection as consciousness itself. This is why the root of consciousness has been called, paradoxically, the unconscious."[23]

Given this, it is a sound philosophy that the esotericist who wishes to explore the primordial realm should do so with primordial methods, those techniques that have long served to tether the incarnate Spiritist to the realm of fleshless forms.

That the esotericist even acknowledges that there are realms, powers, sentient things that lie outside of his or herself is a quality that immediately puts them out of step with the utterly secular modern age, which has lost its connection to the sublime. It is this Poetic Sense, this awareness of that which dwells just beneath the surface of the apparent, that may grant one insight into the Otherworld. This orientation toward that-which-is-not-self, as opposed to modernity's solipsism that insinuates that all-is-self, is a necessity that may broaden the Moribund Portal.

There is something of a slippery paradox here as well, for it seems that as civilization diverges ever-further from the spectral realm, the more startlingly strange, the more Other, the spectral realm becomes to common sensibilities. It is only after extensive work and proper

23 *The Book* by Alan Watts. Pantheon. (1966)

attuning of one's self to achieve Spectral Resonance, that one comes to truly appreciate the sublime that is present *within* these hoary, seemingly unwholesome places. The grotesque is the language of that which dwells beneath the surface of the apparent. To wit, the *Kularnavatantra* espouses, "One reaches heaven by the very things that may lead to hell."[24]

This sense of a greater world that extends beyond one's own perception and exists independently transmutes the seemingly coincidental into portents. The randomness that comforts or bolsters the contemporary materialist is seen by the esotericist as the vast cycle that it truly is.

To experience the Otherworld in the present is to comprehend the inescapable flow of Wyrd, to understand that while one's actions can indeed be chosen as 'free will' decisions, there is an unfathomable momentum of Fate that, when discovered, appreciated, and explored, can be used as the current that pushes one deeper into the Mysteries than any egoic grandstanding against the gods could ever hope to accomplish. Working in harmony with the larger Wheel of Fate is another method by which one proves their worth, their willingness to orient themselves more toward the Spectral Resonance of past unto present and present unto past, rather than hitching themselves to the speeding train of progress and egoism that is whisking the bulk of humankind toward the pipedream of their sterile

24 *Kularnavatantra.*

future of steel, light, and artificial (in more than one sense) intelligence.

To demonstrate how one might begin to orient themselves in a Spiritist manner, we shall return to the notion of seeing the shape of the Agliz and Wunjo runes within the construct of a typical gallows. How might one test such similarities? How might the heft and substance of such apprehensions be assessed to distinguish them from any superficial similarities, such as pareidolia? One method would be to examine the underlying meanings of the *specific* signs or portents one senses, in this case a pair of runes, and determine how these meanings might relate (or not) to the broader concept at hand, in this instance, the Hanging Place as a place of Spirit Power and the sublime.

Agliz is a protection rune and as preeminent runologist Edred Thorsson postulates, its design could be indicative of the splayed human hand.[25] Furthermore, Algiz connects to the Gothic word *alhs*, which means 'sacred grove' or 'enclosure' protected by the gods.[26]

Wunjo represents the invisible but tenacious bond that stretches between two seemingly discrete energies. It is a binding rune in that it harmonizes but does not unify or meld polarities. This harmonizing bolsters these two powers, allowing them to work in tandem toward a singular purpose. Such is the essence of magic; a precise

25 *Futhark: A Handbook of Rune Magic* by Edred Thorsson. Weiser Books. San Francisco. 1984.
26 Ibid.

alignment of elements. Disparate parts operating within a sacred enclosure where all distractions and profanity have been left beyond the rim of the Working space. The bond symbolized by Wunjo may be experienced in the numinous ambiance of the gallows, for by operating within the Hanging Place, one can experience the bond that exists between the noose, the gnarled tree, the crossroads, and the powers that lend them their haunted air. There is recognition from the Otherworld and such implements serve as beacons to draw the Spirits of Place about you. The numen of the gallows recognizes the tools that are indigenous to its site.

The commandments borne by Moses were constrictive, the runes carried back by Odin were expansive. Moses limited his people so that they may know transcendent joys post-mortem. Odin brought forth endless Mystery that could be seen in every patch of woods, heard in every moaning wind, felt as one's hackles were raised when faced with the reality of their Fate, their Wyrd.

What seized Odin on that Ninth Night was not serene enlightenment, but a divine madness. In ancient Greece this phenomenon was known as *telestikós*, 'telestic madness,'[27] the kind of furious, overpowering ecstasy that came from direct knowledge of the primordial. Odin was the very embodiment of telestic madness in Norse history. His name means 'Master of Ecstasy,' or 'Furious One'; titles that emphasize the frenzied,

27 See *Phaedrus* by Plato.

elemental nature of his wisdom. The runes were not some inert formula. In fact, when Odin received them, the runes were described as howling; indicative of their fearsome, vital, and unworldly potency.

The Mysteries of the runes linger and resound wherever and whenever they appear. While the reader is advised to independently explore the implications between this pair of runes and the numen of the gallows, suffice it to say that when such signs are not only noticed but actualized, the process of Mystery leading one unto greater Mystery is invited.

Odin was not the stoic intellectual, doling out gems of advice to a circle of rapt students. He was the afflicted, one-eyed madman, whose self-awareness could be shared only by those who dared to follow his example.

Many may seek the glories of initiation, but relatively few are willing to pay its toll. Glory only comes to those who push themselves beyond their own limitations, both spiritually and physically.

To illustrate that the nature of Odin's self-sacrifice was not some pallid literary metaphor for soul-searching or some other psychological model, one may look to the O-Kee-pa ceremony of the Mandan tribe of what became North and South Dakota, USA. The O-Kee-pa was said to have been an exhaustive affair that culminated with the young men of the tribe voluntarily suspending themselves by way of having incisions made in their chest through which corded splints were implanted. These cords would then be used to hoist the men above the ground. There, bloodied and dazed, the men would invariably faint from the sheer excruciating pain of their suspension. Dangling limp and unconscious, these men "had, in each instance, the appearance of a corpse."[28] Finally, they would be lowered to the ground, where none of the tribesmen or women were permitted to touch them until their consciousness was restored.

This trying ordeal was undertaken so that the hanged ones could come to experience the Great Spirit of their faith. As painter and historian George Catlin noted upon observing the unconscious men,

> They were here enjoying their inestimable privilege of voluntarily entrusting to the keeping of the Great Spirit, and chose to remain there until the Great Spirit gave them strength to get up and walk away.[29]

¶

WHAT RADIATES FROM the Hanging Place is the shadow that precedes the form, the umbra that is not the mere reflection of the material articulation but is the manifestation of the veiled process of dream into form. This process flowers according to the orientation of the individual. The transubstantiation of dream occurs when the witness first apprehends the numinous

28 *O-Kee-pa: A Religious Ceremony; and Other Customs of the Mandans* by George Catlin. J. B. Lippincott & Co. Philadelphia. 1867.
29 Ibid.

shadow-essence of that which they are witnessing and follows this with the drawing forth of this foundational shadow-essence via the precise tuning of intuition and desire. These twain powers, when invoked in equal measure, create the precious vibration that opens the Moribund Portal.

Learn well the art of radiating the specificity of your intention. Become that which you desire, and in due course the *Fylgja* that doubles your own waking vessel shall shower your every mortal thought and worldly action with outré boons.

The essence of this kind of power is indigenous to liminality, in this case, the liminality that is the spore of earnest contemplation and exploration of the masked, and therefore identity-less, form who no longer walks the earth as one of the living, yet whose lifeless remains have earned no state of graceful burial nor shows any signs of celestial admittance. The Hanged One quite literally becomes a Thing; be it an emblem of local jurisprudence, a macabre warning to not venture too far past the borderlands, a repository of magical tools, such as seed and hand.

The physical suspension of the body between earth and sky has been shown as a means of admission into a liminal state of being, but this process also has an immaterial counterpart, a means of absolute reorientation of one's reckoning of time and space. The Portal does not open for all, and while sacrifice is not guaranteed to be accepted, it is unquestionably a meritorious act that is more likely to enhance one's chances than not.

What is of paramount importance is the proper orientation of time reckoning. One should perceive themselves as being stationed at a pole that is the present. Cast one's attention into one's own depths until the timeless Well of Urd is apprehended. Maintenance of this model of time reckoning will aid one in the broadening of the Moribund Portal. These are the two poles that reside in the wilderness as the crossroads and that loom in semiotics as the two poles of the *galgon,* the cosmic gallows, the Mysteries of the Gebo rune actualized.

Inroads toward the Otherworld can be successfully forged by employing the hangman's noose to "sacrifice" the sorcerous tools of hand and eye. Cinching the loop of the noose around the wrist of one's writing hand, a hand adorned with glyphs drawn from dream and trance, impinging the circulation to the primary hand, creates the receptive state.

One's eye should remain transfixed upon the array of fetishes that fill the Working site. Offer these to the Spirits to use as They wish. The result will be automatic writings and the ghostly figures of trance.

The numen and attendant spirits of the gallows all recognize the implements indigenous to this place (the noose, the mandrake root, the timeless and almost skeletal tree, et al.) and gravitate toward them. What's more, their connection to these tools, and by extension the visitant who bears them, is icily detached. It is not an emotive recognition, but the recognition of the Moribund Portal.

Epilogue

To go wayfaring, to bask in the gloom of neglected places. To undertake excursions at eventide, or deep in the night; solitarily, silently.

To hunt for the obscured patch that raises hackles, births shudders.

Vision thereby erupts; unbridled, vital as coursing blood. This is the imagistic language of Others. But just as in days of old, payment must be made to these storytellers.

A rope whose braid was spun counter-clockwise, in keeping with the hangman's custom, is slung over the limb of a tree of imposing stature and shape. Beneath this, the alraune fumes pungently, its smoke to serve as skin for the unseen.

Dusk thickens. Offerings and fetishes are reverentially stationed between tree roots, upon standing stone.

A low-burning lamp gutters, the sole means of illumination, save for the pale lustre of moonlight. As the lamp fire wanes, the sparks and flickers of ghost-lights may at last be perceived.

Here, modernity is but a faint wisp of memory. Within the sacred enclosure are only those items that are recognizable to both the enfleshed and the disincarnated of the Otherworld. These objects drip with echoes of the deep past, which is in truth the timeless. They are the keys that unlock the gates to nocturnal Eden.

Storm the gates and See.

See...

See the noose dangling like a pendulum. The noose shall serve as your focal point, as the mirror does the scryer. One looks upon this as they do their *Fylgja* in a dream; not through direct gaze but peripherally, poetically. This, the tried and true mode of Seership, stirs the ethereal fog, the mist that congeals in the vacant loop of the noose; the Circle that becomes the Moribund Portal.

When the poles of past and present fall in line, the deep harmonic tone shall resound throughout the enclosure. The trees may also shiver as the chorus of the Dead rises. The gallows birds shall take flight from their nests.

The noose swings, twists, flexes, indeed dances. Ghost-lights spark as brilliantly as jewels within the surrounding shadows. But these glints are but a projected mask of certain spirits. Their true appearance, if unveiled as in the legend of *La Corriveau*, unwaveringly terrifies. I have borne witness to misshapen skeletal forms skittering about groves and dragging themselves across charnel grounds. The reader may consider themselves forewarned.

As the past flows into the present and the present pours into the past, savour that which passes before you and through you. Safeguard these boons, for their worth is far greater than any worldly treasure. This is the imagistic grammar of your Wyrd.

Each of us is being drawn, inexorably drawn, toward a waiting grave and boons such as this serve as precious waymarks. They illuminate our way back to the timeless enclosure, even after we have moved on to join the shadow-company on the opposite side of the Moribund Portal.

Acknowledgements

The author wishes to express his gratitude to the following for their assistance and support toward this monograph's creation: Kaitlin Coppock, Holly Dunk, James Dunk, Robert Fitzgerald, David Beth & Jessica Grote, Lora Lagan, Daniel A. Schulke, Joseph Uccello, and Benjamin A. Vierling.

BIBLIOGRAPHY

Druce, George C. (trans.) *British Library Harley Manuscript 4986*, 12th Century CE.

Geroge Catlin, *O-Kee-pa: A Religious Ceremony; and Other Customs of the Mandans*. J. B. Lippincott & Co. Philadelphia, 1867.

Donne, John. *Metempsychosis: Poêma Satyricon*.

Flavius Josephus, *The History of the Jewish War against the Romans*. (Various editions.), 78 CE.

Frazer, J. G. *Jacob and the Mandrakes*. Oxford University Press. Oxford, 1917.

Herodotus. *Histories*. (Various editions.) 440 CE.

Holinshead, Raphael. *Holinshead's Chronicles*, 1586.

Holy Bible, King James Edition.

Homer. *The Odyssey*. (Samuel Butler, trans.), 1898.

Kulārṇavatantra. (Various editions)

Lucian of Samosata *A True Story*. (A. M. Harmon trans.) G. P. Putnam & Sons. New York, 1913.

Plato. *Phaedrus* (Various editions).

Pliny the Elder (79 CE). *Natural History*.

Schulke, Daniel A. (2005) *Viridarium Umbris: The Pleasure Garden of Shadow*. Xoanon Publishing. UK.

Secrets merveilleux de la magie naturelle et cabalistique du Petit Albert, 1752.

Skeat, William Walter. *Notes on English Etymology*. Clarendon Press. Oxford, 1904.

Spare, Austin Osman. *The Book of Pleasure (Self Love): The Psychology of Ecstasy*. London, 1913.

The Herbarium of Apuleius, 400 CE.

Thorsson, Edred. *Futhark: A Handbook of Rune Magic*. Weiser Books. San Francisco, 1984.

—*The Mysteries of the Goths*. Runa-Raven Press. Smithville, 2007.

Watts, Alan. *The Book: On the Taboo Against Knowing Who You Are*. Pantheon, New York, 1966.

¶

The Moribund Portal was printed & bound at Walpurgisnacht, 2018 in an edition of two thousand two hundred twenty-two impressions. Of these are 1,700 softcover copies, 500 hand-numbered hardcover copies in tyrian purple cloth, and 22 hand-numbered deluxe copies in full purple Nigerian goat with slip-case. Fine bindings executed by The Key Printing & Binding, Oakland, California.

SCRIBÆ QUO MYSTERIUM FAMULATUR